D1281458

HUMPTY DUMPTY

and Other Nursery Rhymes

illustrated by Rod Ruth

A Golden Book • New York

Western Publishing Company, Inc.
Racine, Wisconsin 53404

Humpty Dumpty sat on a wall;
Humpty Dumpty had a great fall.
All the king's horses
    and all the king's men
Couldn't put Humpty together again.

Mary had a little lamb;
Its fleece was white as snow,
And everywhere that Mary went,
The lamb was sure to go.

He followed her to school one day,
Which was against the rule.
It made the children laugh and play
To see a lamb in school.

And so the teacher turned him out,
But still he lingered near
And waited patiently about
Till Mary did appear.

"What makes the lamb love Mary so?"
The eager children cried.
"Oh, Mary loves the lamb, you know,"
The teacher then replied.

Pat-a-cake, pat-a-cake, baker's man!
Bake me a cake as fast as you can.
Roll it and pat it and mark it with *B*,
And put it in the oven for baby and me.

Jack Sprat could eat no fat,
His wife could eat no lean;
And so, between them both, you see,
They licked the platter clean.

Twinkle, twinkle, little star.
How I wonder what you are,
Up above the world so high,
Like a diamond in the sky.

Jack, be nimble;
Jack, be quick;
Jack, jump over the candlestick!

There was a crooked man, and he went
a crooked mile.
He found a crooked sixpence against
a crooked stile.
He bought a crooked cat, which caught
a crooked mouse,
And they all lived together in a little
crooked house.

Little Boy Blue, come blow your horn!
The sheep's in the meadow,
The cow's in the corn.

Where is the boy who looks after
    the sheep?
He's under the haystack, fast asleep.
Will you wake him? No, not I,
For if I do, he'll surely cry.

Old King Cole was a merry old soul,
And a merry old soul was he.
He called for his pipe,
He called for his bowl,
And he called for his fiddlers three.

Every fiddler, he had a fiddle,
And a very fine fiddle had he.
Tweedle dee, tweedle dee
   went the fiddlers three.
Oh, there's none so rare
As can compare
With King Cole and his fiddlers three.

Hey, diddle, diddle,
The cat and the fiddle.
The cow jumped over the moon!
The little dog laughed to see such sport,
And the dish ran away with the spoon.

Little Jack Horner sat in the corner
Eating a Christmas pie;
He put in his thumb and pulled out a plum
And said, "What a good boy am I!"

Little Bo-Peep has lost her sheep
And can't tell where to find them.
Leave them alone, and they'll come home
Wagging their tails behind them.

Hickory, dickory, dock,
The mouse ran up the clock.
The clock struck one;
The mouse ran down,
Hickory, dickory, dock.

Sing a song of sixpence,
A pocket full of rye,
Four and twenty blackbirds
Baked in a pie.

When the pie was opened,
The birds began to sing.
Wasn't that a dainty dish
To set before a king?

The king was in the countinghouse
Counting out his money;
The queen was in the parlor
Eating bread and honey.

The maid was in the garden
Hanging out the clothes,
When down came a blackbird
And snipped off her nose.

Where, oh, where has my little dog gone?
Oh, where, oh, where can he be?
With his tail so short
    and his ears so long—
Oh, where, oh, where can he be?

Rain, rain, go away.
Come again another day;
Little Tommy wants to play.

A little old woman lived under a hill;
And if she's not gone, she lives there still.

Once I saw a little bird
Come hop, hop, hop,
So I cried, "Little bird,
Will you stop, stop, stop?"

I was going to the window
To say, "How do you do?"
But he shook his little tail,
And far away he flew.

Diddle, diddle, dumpling, my son John,
He went to bed with his stockings on;
One shoe off and one shoe on;
Diddle, diddle, dumpling, my son John.

There were two blackbirds
Sitting on a hill—
The one named Jack,
The other named Jill.
Fly away, Jack! Fly away, Jill!
Come again, Jack! Come again, Jill!